Turning Back to Allah

Sulaiman's Caving Calamity

By
Aliya Vaughan

THE ISLAMIC
FOUNDATION

Turning Back to Allah – Sulaiman's Caving Calamity

First Published in 2021 by
THE ISLAMIC FOUNDATION

Distributed by
KUBE PUBLISHING LTD
Tel +44 (0)1530 249230, Fax +44 (0)1530 249656
E-mail: info@kubepublishing.com
Website: www.kubepublishing.com

Text copyright © Aliya Vaughan, 2021
Illustrations copyright © Rakaiya Azzouz, 2021

All rights reserved. No part of this publication may be reproduced, stored in a retrieval system, or transmitted in any form or by any means, electronic, mechanical, photocopying, recording or otherwise, without the prior permission of the copyright owner

Author Aliya Vaughan
Illustrator Rakaiya Azzouz
Book design Rebecca Wildman

A Cataloguing-in-Publication Data record for this book is available from the British Library

ISBN 978-0-86037-840-2
eISBN 978-0-86037-845-7

Printed in Turkey by Elma Printing.

Contents

Note to Parents..5

Chapter 1...7

Chapter 2...11

Chapter 3...16

Chapter 4...21

Chapter 5...28

Chapter 6...41

Comprehension Questions...50

"And remember Yunus (Jonah) when he went off in anger, and thought We would not punish him! But he cried through the darkness saying '*Laa ilaaha illa anta*. Truly I have been of the wrong-doers.'

So, We answered his call, and delivered him from distress. And thus, We do deliver the believers."

Surah al-Anbiya 21:87-88

Note to reader and parents

Turning Back to Allah is an exciting story for children about a young Muslim boy who learns the importance of sincere du'a and reliance on Allah by turning back to Him at all times and asking for help and forgiveness.

Allah loves us to call upon Him and to ask of Him, and He loves to answer our du'as (supplications).
It says in the Qur'an, *Surah Ghaafir* (also known as *Surah al-Mu'min*) verse number sixty: "And your Lord said: 'Pray to Me, and I will accept your prayers.'"

Chapter 1

"It's like I'm walking on toast!" Sulaiman laughed, as the dry leaves crunched beneath his trainers. He grabbed a huge handful from beneath the tree and heaped them on top of Hannah's head.

"My hair!" she cried, bending over and flicking them off. One rebellious little leaf escaped down the back of her shirt collar. She wriggled up and down to free it.

"You wait!" she growled, and swinging her bag high above her head she chased him all the way up to the flat. Sulaiman quickly swiped his card across the intercom keypad and waited by the lift.

"Race you!" Sulaiman shouted playfully, "You take the lift. I'll take the stairs." Sulaiman competed with his sister in just about everything, from arm wrestling to computer games and even tying up their shoe laces. But this bet was about more than just winning a race.

Sulaiman refused to take the lift after getting trapped between two floors last summer. It was a really hot day and he had been caged in with his neighbour's stinky armpits and grumpy Yorkshire terrier for hours. His dad called the firemen to rescue them, but he never fully recovered from the ordeal. He sprinted up three flights of

stairs and peered down the stairwell. Hannah was just stepping inside the lift. "Only two more floors to go, I can still make it," he wagered, running up to the fifth and final floor with clenched teeth. The lift door was just sliding open.

He barged past Hannah as she was coming out and skidded up to the front door. "I won!" he boasted.

"Yeah? But I'm gonna be first in the flat," she insisted and brushed past him to insert her key into the lock.

"You're just a sore loser," Sulaiman teased, prodding her arm.

Chapter 2

That night Sulaiman was preparing for his weekend trip. "Two jumpers, three trousers, three pairs of socks…" He ticked the items on his list one by one and packed them into his backpack.

"Why can't I come with you?" Hannah whined as she trampolined on her knees on Sulaiman's bed. Her ponytail rose and fell with every bounce.

"Because Scouts are for boys," Sulaiman taunted. "No, they're not! Safia's going with the Girl Scouts."

"Well, you still can't come because you'll get scared in the cave," he teased. Hannah grabbed a rolled-up pair of socks from his backpack and threw it hard. It skimmed past Sulaiman's ducked head and knocked some toys off the bookshelf behind him.

"Okay, prove you're not scared then, get in the wardrobe," he demanded.

As Hannah stepped inside the wardrobe, Sulaiman quickly locked the door behind her. Her ear-piercing screams and banging brought their dad running from the next room. "Sulaiman!" he barked, unlocking the door to let her out. "You didn't like it when she locked *you* in there last week, did you?" The colour drained from Sulaiman's face as he remembered how dark it was, not

being able to see or hear anything. "Sorry." He muttered reluctantly under his breath.

Hannah ran into her dad's comforting arms and sobbed loudly for extra dramatic effect and to gain more sympathy. When her dad wasn't looking, she tried to stomp on Sulaiman's foot in revenge. Sulaiman was oblivious to her provocation as he was now deep in thought and peering nervously inside his backpack. Dad sensed he was having second thoughts about his trip and tried to reassure him. "Don't worry; it won't be like that time in the park. You'll have caving instructors to look after you. Have you packed everything you need?" Sulaiman took another look inside his backpack. "I haven't got a helmet or a torch…" he fussed, "…or waterproof clothes."

"They'll give you all that when you get there," said Dad calmly, and handed him a towel and bag of toiletries. Sulaiman rolled up his sleeping bag tightly into its casing, then fastened it securely on top of his backpack. "Get ready for bed now. You've got an early start tomorrow," his dad reminded him. It was usually a mission getting Sulaiman to go to bed on time, but not tonight. He accepted his dad's orders willingly.

Chapter 3

Early the next morning Sulaiman met up with the other Scouts to go on their caving trip. He boarded the mini bus and sat next to his friend, Jacob. As they drove off, Sulaiman looked a little pale.

"What's the matter, have you forgotten something?" Jacob asked. Sulaiman shook his head.

"Can I sit next to the window?"

"Urgh, why, do you get travel sick?" Jacob cringed and quickly grabbed a paper bag from the front seat pocket. Sulaiman pushed it away from his face and sniggered.

"No. I need to read the signposts," he explained. Jacob stared at Sulaiman through his messy blonde strands of hair, looking puzzled. "You need a better reason than that if you want me to give up my seat," he insisted. Sulaiman hesitated and fidgeted awkwardly but he really wanted to see the signs. Choosing his words carefully, he rolled his eyes and took in a deep breath.

"Okay. When I was four, I was at the park..." Jacob waited for Sulaiman to continue but he stopped mid-sentence.

"And...?" Jacob nodded, "So, what happened?"

"I got lost, okay!" Sulaiman whispered with a grimace. He glanced sideways to

make sure no one had overheard him. "It was getting dark and a security man threatened to lock me in. But it was no big deal, my mum and dad found me in the end."

"So why do you need to read the signposts?" Jacob asked looking even more confused.

"To know which way to go if we get lost."

"But we won't get lost! The driver knows where we're going," Jacob teased.

"I mean if we get lost in the cave," Sulaiman whispered feebly. Jacob stared at him for a few seconds and then his eyes widened. "Ohhh… I get it," nodded Jacob knowingly and quickly reassured him.

"It's okay, you won't get lost. We'll stick together like glue, alright?" Sulaiman was relieved Jacob hadn't made fun of him. He hated being scared of the dark and was glad Jacob would be close by.

Chapter 4

It took a few hours to drive to the hostel. To pass the time, the boys amused themselves with witty stories and games.

As they drove along the motorway, Sulaiman stared in awe at the rolling green hills and countryside. It was so different to the busy, bustling city he had left behind.

"Eww! Open a window!" Sulaiman shouted covering his nose with his jumper.

"No don't!" Jacob yelled leaning across Sulaiman to stop him pulling on the window latch. "It's coming from outside. It must be a farm!"

"I think I'm gonna faint," Sulaiman groaned. He forced his head inside the sick bag and pretended to gag. "I'm never complaining about the pollution in the city again."

Several hours later, after coming off the motorway they drove through a village hamlet. It was similar to one you would see on a pretty, picture postcard. Sulaiman suddenly noticed a sign on a village green by a duck pond.

"I think we're here!" he cried, nudging Jack from his sleep. He accidentally spilt his drink down Jacob's trousers.

"Oh, thanks!" Jacob moaned, looking down onto his lap. "Now it looks like I've

wet myself!"

"We're here! Look," Sulaiman cried tugging on Jacob's jumper excitedly.

They passed a row of cottages and a grocery shop, travelled over a narrow bridge by a church and a railway station, until they eventually turned into a long gravel drive with overhanging trees.

"This must be where we're staying," Sulaiman exclaimed pointing to the large wooden lodge at the end. "I can't wait to go exploring." The lodge owner greeted them at the reception desk and showed them to their rooms. For the next two days, Sulaiman and his fellow Scouts would be sharing a dormitory with bunk beds.

"This one's mine," Sulaiman insisted and threw his backpack onto a top bunk.

"The last time I slept on a bottom bunk, it collapsed on me!" Jacob quickly threw his backpack onto another top bunk so they could face each other.

"G'day boys!" a voice bellowed. A large figure swung into the room from the top of the doorframe, taking the boys by surprise. One of them smacked his head on the bedframe. "Oi! Mind'ya nose!" he laughed, ruffling the boy's hair in fun. Lucas was their Scout leader. He was an energetic, young man with a very loud, Australian accent.

"Unpack'ya stuff, then come to the reception desk," Lucas instructed, "You've got ten minutes. If ya're late, I'll leave without'ya and eat all'ya food." The boys grabbed their bags in a frantic, flurry of excitement and tossed their belongings inside the wardrobes and drawers.

Once Lucas had taken the register, they all boarded the mini bus and drove off to the training centre.

"Listen carefully to what the instructors tell'ya," Lucas warned, "Ya need to be safe inside the caves. If it floods or'ya get lost, you need to know what to do, ya'hear?"

Sulaiman and the boys were given a talk about caving safety, and were then shown how to put on their safety harnesses for the obstacle assault course. That afternoon they climbed up and down ropes over brick walls, crawled through tunnels, slid down zip-slides and scrambled over logs in muddy ditches. It was a very messy, exciting afternoon.

"Oi, look at the state of'ya!" Lucas groaned when they returned back to the lodge. The boys were caked in mud from head to foot.

"Ya can't come in here looking like that! Leave'ya coats and boots by the back door. We'll bash the mud off when its dried in the morning."

"I think I got mud in my ears!" Jacob sniggered shaking his head from side to side. "I can bash them for you too, if you want?" Sulaiman joked pulling hard on his lobes. They quickly shed their outer garments and ran upstairs to the dorms. After freshening up and changing into clean clothes, they joined the rest of the group in the dining room for dinner.

Once they had eaten and tidied up, they played team games until bed time. Although they enjoyed the day, they couldn't wait to explore a *real* cave. The best was still yet to come.

Chapter 5

After breakfast the next day, the boys set off to the training centre again. It was a cold, frosty morning but they had wrapped up warm, wearing plenty of thin layers of clothing. The caving instructors handed the boys the equipment they would need for their exploration in the cave. Sulaiman zipped himself into a green, waterproof suit with a harness. As he pulled at the straps

they tightened around his arms and legs, until he couldn't move.

"You look like a frog!" Jacob howled as he watched Sulaiman hop around the room trying to free himself.

"Help me then!" Sulaiman begged as he squirmed and wriggled up and down. But Jacob showed no mercy and laughed even harder. Lucas eventually had to step in to untangle him.

"How d'ya get like that?" he smirked, and handed Sulaiman a helmet with a cap lamp on the front. The caving instructors packed all the safety equipment into their backpacks and checked their two-way radios. They then began the short trek to the caves.

It was a breath-taking sight. They walked through a wooded hillside rising above the river. There was a light mist hovering half way above the trees making the atmosphere feel creepy and mysterious.

"It's like that time I got lost in the park," Sulaiman remembered shuddering to himself. He was glad he wasn't alone.

The river continued to wind through a narrow gorge with steep rocky cliffs until they came to a clearing in the wood. It no longer felt creepy, instead it was enchanting and magical. The mist had vanished and streams of hazy sunlight shone through the branches of the trees.

"Look over there!" pointed Sulaiman towards the entrance of a cave. Its massive, menacing mouth was beckoning them to enter. Suddenly, high-pitched squeaks and fluttering was heard overhead as bats flew out of the darkness into the bright, autumn sunlight.

"They're gonna hit me!" shrieked Jacob, falling to his knees. He wrapped his arms tightly around his head to protect himself. Peering out from under his helmet, he checked to see if any more were coming.

"It's okay, they've gone," Sulaiman laughed helping Jacob back onto his feet.

Lucas was standing at the entrance of the cave explaining how the caves had formed millions of years ago, dating back to the Ice Age. Sulaiman and Jacob moved closer to the front to hear what he had to say. Lucas waved his arms to describe the caves in lively detail. The boys had already learnt a lot about caves in lessons at school, but Lucas was far more entertaining.

"Turn on'ya headlamps," Lucas instructed when he had finished his talk. As they entered the cave, the light quickly faded until all that could be seen were beams of light from the group's headlamps.

Jacob swung his head from side to side to create sweeping patterns of light across the cave wall. Sulaiman copied him and soon there were light beams dancing and overlapping one another at speed. "Steady boys, you'll get dizzy," Lucas joked. The sniggering pair nudged each other mischievously.

The group ventured further inside the cave, scrambling over boulders and up past narrow passageways. Soon, the archways got lower and lower until they led onto some beautifully decorated chambers. The walls and ceilings were covered with amazing stalactites, curtains and formations.

The group stood to admire them as Lucas continued his talk. "These underground chambers are naturally formed by water flowing through the cracks in the limestone. Over time, the rock has dissolved and eroded to produce the caverns we see today…" Sulaiman took off his backpack and searched through a side pocket for his camera. He focused the lens on an overhanging stalactite glistening in the beam of his headlamp. A pearly, white stalagmite had formed directly underneath it, where limestone deposits had dripped onto the cave floor and hardened. He took a few snapshots, then admired them on the viewing screen.

Just then, a little orange light started to flash on his camera. It was indicating that the batteries were low. He was glad he had packed some spare ones and hastily retrieved them from his backpack.

As Sulaiman ripped open the packaging, the batteries spilled out onto the floor. He quickly bent down to pick them up again. Lucas's voice could still be heard in the

background.

"The Greek word for drip is stalagmatia. A stalactite grows approximately one centimetre every two hundred years…"

As Sulaiman counted the batteries in his hand, he noticed one of them was missing. He shone his headlamp across the cave floor to find it. A shiny gold object glinted in the light through a crack between a boulder and the cave wall.

Sulaiman kneeled down and thrust his arm through the gap. He tried to grab it, but it was slightly out of reach.

"What are you doing?" Jacob whispered, peering over Sulaiman's hunched body to get a better look.

"I lost my battery. Help me get it out, will you?" Jacob lay flat on the ground and tried to reach it with his outstretched hand. "I can't. It's gone too far in," he grunted. "Have you got a belt?" Sulaiman suggested, "We could get it out with that."

Jacob quickly unzipped his caving suit, and wrestled to remove his belt from his trousers. "I hope it's long enough." Sulaiman grabbed the belt and beat the buckle end onto the battery through the gap. With every stroke, the battery rolled bit by bit towards him.

"Got it!" Sulaiman cried finally. He opened the battery door to his camera and slotted it inside. The flashing light quickly switched from orange to green.

"I can take a few more pictures now." He smiled, glancing back at Jacob, but Jacob had disappeared. He also noticed that the chamber was now eerily quiet. He could no longer hear Lucas's voice or see the lights from the other headlamps.

"Where's everybody gone?" Sulaiman

panicked. He ran to the end of the chamber next to an iron railing that was hammered into the rock. It was fencing off a large hole in the ground.

"They must have gone down this pothole, there's no other way out," he thought shining his headlamp down the pothole pitch to get a better look.

"I could follow them down this rope ladder." But then he remembered what the instructors had said if they got lost. He slumped onto the floor with his head in his hands. He knew he should stay where he was, but it was dark and cold and he was starting to get hungry and thirsty.

"Jacob promised we'd stick together like glue," he tutted in frustration. Just then the light from Sulaiman's headlamp began to flicker.

"Oh no! It can't pack up now!"

He freaked, smacking the side of his helmet with the palm of his hand. "Maybe it's a loose connection."

The light flickered and faded to a faint glow and then suddenly disappeared altogether. He was now in complete darkness. He glanced wide-eyed in every direction, towards all the strange and unusual noises.

He could hear water dripping from the ceiling and bats squeaking from above. He shivered nervously. He reached out to grab the iron railing next to the pothole, but it was dark and he couldn't see it properly. Getting up onto his feet, he slowly shuffled forward waving his hands out in front of him. After taking a few steps, he suddenly stumbled sideways, hitting his head hard against the low rock ceiling and fell to the floor.

He lay lifeless on the cold, damp ground.

A beetle scurried over his hand to feed on some bat droppings close by. It was just as well he hadn't felt it, as it would have made him panic even more.

Chapter 6

After several minutes, Sulaiman slowly regained consciousness. His head was throbbing and he could feel the warmth of his blood trickling down his temple.

He suddenly remembered where he was and that he was still all alone.

"What if they never find me?" he fretted, remembering the time he got lost in the park. "What if I get bitten by a vampire bat or starve to death?"

He pushed himself up and leaned against a nearby boulder. It was getting colder so he buried his head into his knees and drew them up to his chest to keep warm. He sighed heavily and wanted to cry but shook the negative thoughts from his head.

"It reminds me of that story when three men got stuck in a cave. A rock blocked the entrance and they couldn't get out," he thought to himself. "They were rescued by Allah when one of them mentioned a good deed they had performed for His sake."

Sulaiman quickly raised his hands in du'a, "Oh Allah, if I cleaned my bedroom for your sake, please rescue me." The light on his head lamp flickered but quickly went out again. "I suppose it doesn't count if my mum told me to do it!" he thought ashamedly. He tried to think of some other

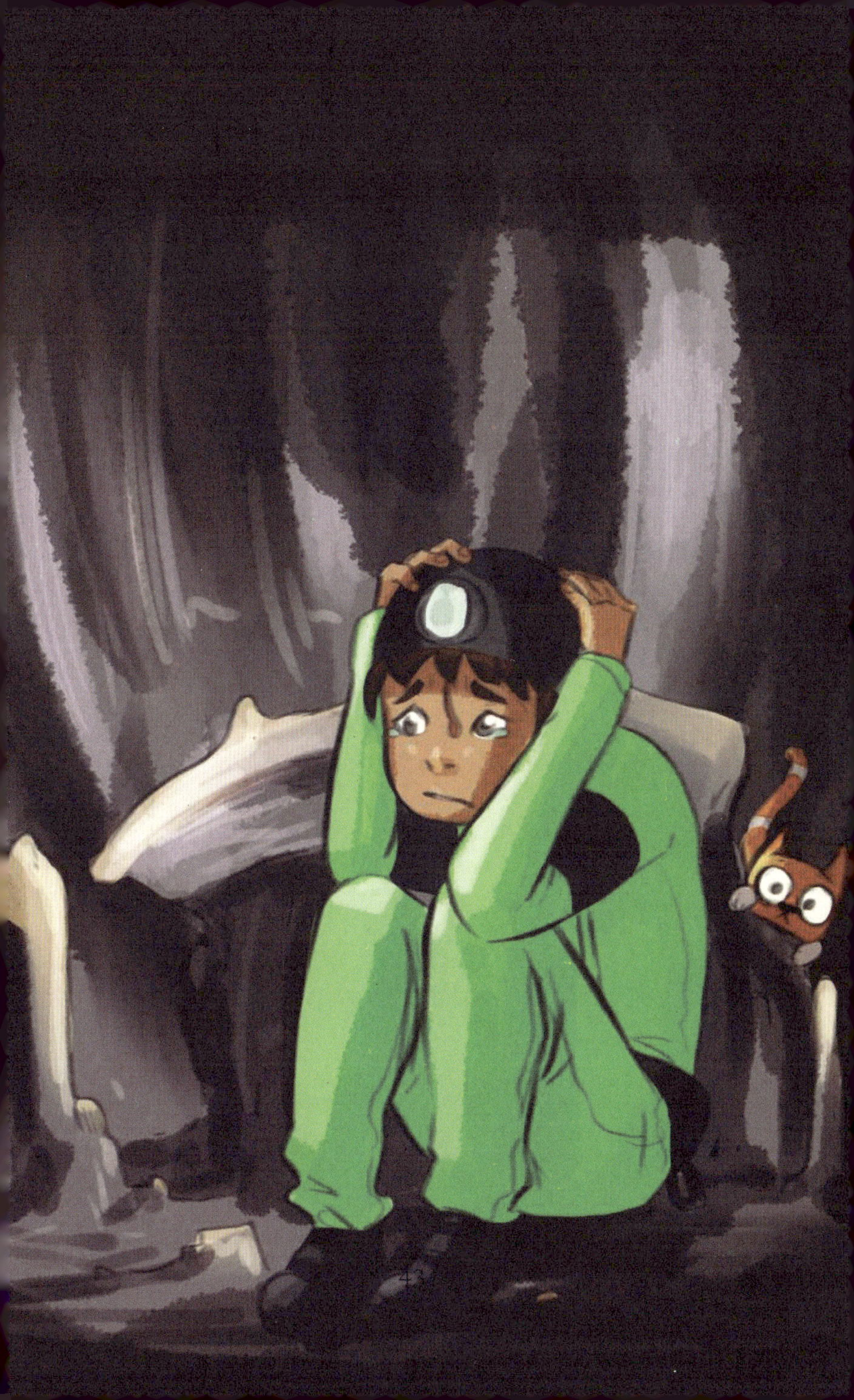

good deeds he had done, but he couldn't remember anything special.

"I need to do more good deeds in future. I can't even rely on somebody else's good deeds as I'm all alone here." He tried to think of another inspiring story that would help him in his lonely time of need. "Prophet Yunus was trapped inside the belly of a whale because he left his people before Allah told him to. He begged Allah to forgive him, then the whale spat him out onto shore and he was saved." Sulaiman tried to think how he could apply the moral of the story to himself.

"Perhaps I need to ask Allah to forgive me," he thought, remembering how horrible he had been to Hannah for locking her inside the wardrobe. Sulaiman raised his hands again and asked Allah sincerely to forgive him.

Suddenly he heard a faint hissing sound like running water. "Oh no! I hope it isn't raining," he panicked, "I'll drown if it floods in here!" In pitch darkness, he scrambled on top of the boulder to save himself. Episodes of his short life flashed before his eyes, as he pictured all the faces of his family and friends.

"What if I never see them again?" His lips trembled and a solitary tear rolled down his soil-stained cheek. Several minutes passed as he sat all alone in the dark.

"Oh, Allah please save me," he pleaded desperately again and again.

Just then, Sulaiman heard faint voices approaching. They began to echo louder and louder from the bottom of the pothole pitch. Wiping his tears, he quickly crawled to the metal railing and peered down the pothole.

The hissing was getting louder and was now more recognisable. He suddenly realised it wasn't rain after all. The sound was, in fact, reception interference on a two-way radio.

Flashes of light flickered off the walls and a beam of light blinded him momentarily as it shone up into his eyes. One of the instructors climbed up the rope ladder, with Lucas climbing up behind him. "Alhamdulillah! (thank God)." Sulaiman repeated over and over again. He was so happy to see them.

"Oh No! What happened?" Lucas asked, turning Sulaiman's head sideways to inspect the wound on his head. Sulaiman told him how he had lost his battery and stayed behind to find it. One of the instructors retrieved a first aid kit from his backpack.

"It's not a deep cut, so I doubt you'll need stitches," he reassured Sulaiman, "I'll put a dressing on it though to protect it from infection." He used an antiseptic wipe to clean the injury and applied a soft, sterile pad, securing it in place with medical tape.

"Did'ya pass out?" Lucas asked looking concerned. "Yeah, I think I did," Sulaiman nodded wearily. "We'd better get'ya checked out at the hospital then. Don't want'ya having concussion."

"But I haven't been down a pothole yet," Sulaiman begged pitifully. Lucas's face softened. He could see how much it meant to him. After all, it was the whole reason for going on the trip.

"No worries mate. There's an amazing pothole coming up in a sec. We'll take a look before we leave, alright?" Sulaiman nodded eagerly. He was happy he hadn't missed out altogether.

One by one, all the boys climbed out of the

pothole and gathered around Sulaiman to see if he was okay. Jacob smiled sheepishly.

"Your glue isn't very sticky, is it?" Sulaiman joked sarcastically.

"Sorry. I thought you were behind me," Jacob explained humbly. "I'll make you a hot chocolate when we get back to the lodge to make up for it."

The thought of a warm drink was just what Sulaiman needed. As they made their way towards the next pothole, Sulaiman noticed Jacob was walking strangely. He was struggling to hold up his trousers under his waterproof suit.

"Can I have my belt back now?" Jacob asked bashfully. Sulaiman gasped and covered his mouth to hide his laughter. He suddenly realised he had left it behind.

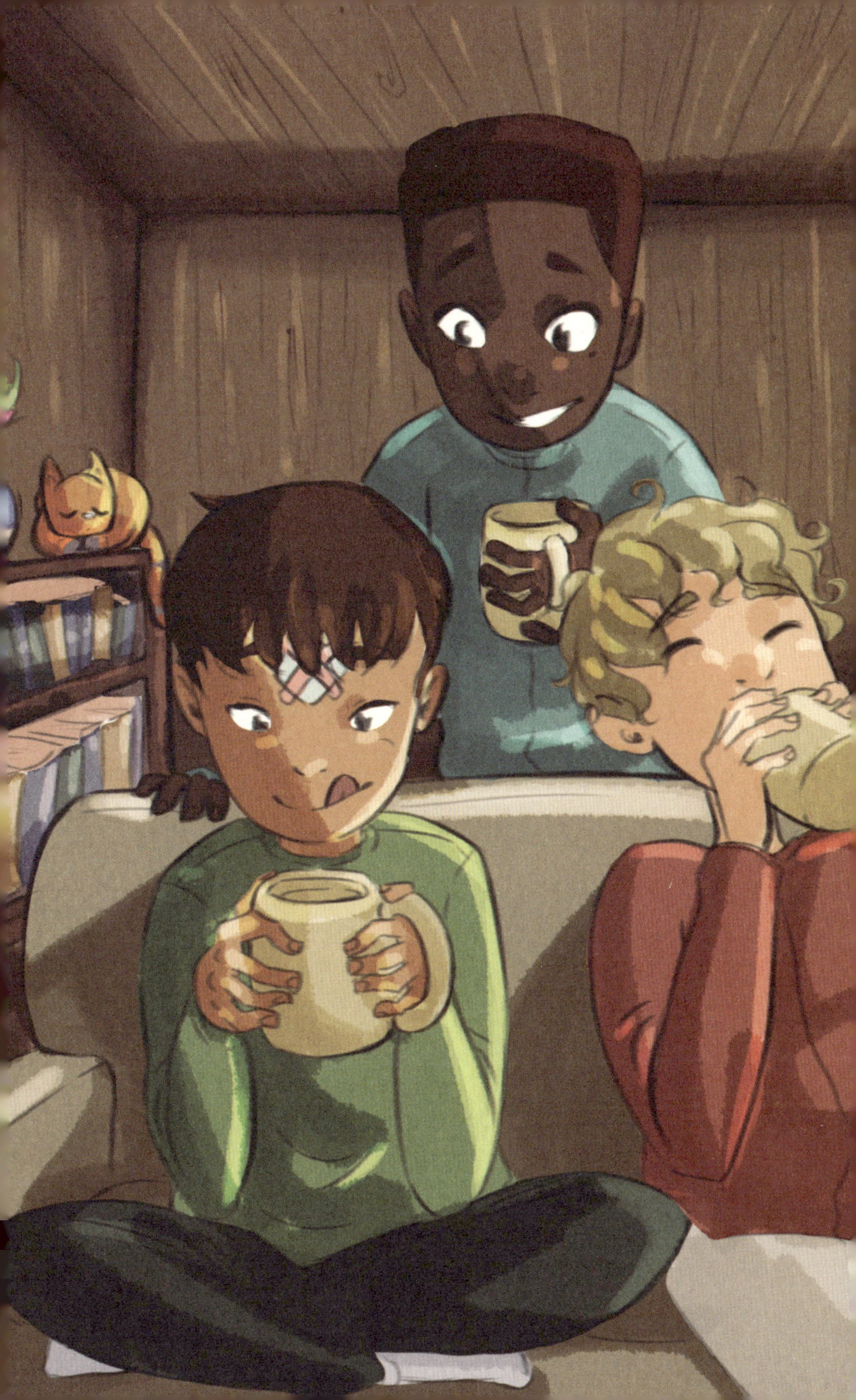

Comprehension Questions

1. Where was Sulaiman going on his Scout trip?

2. Why did Sulaiman want to sit in Jacob's seat next to the window?

3. What was Sulaiman afraid of? What memory caused him to behave like this?

4. Why did Jacob cover his head at the entrance of the cave?

5. How do stalactites and stalagmites form inside caves?

6. How did Sulaiman get left behind?

7. What did Sulaiman use to get the missing battery?

8. Which two stories did Sulaiman remember while he was on his own inside the cave?

9. What did Sulaiman do after remembering the stories?

10. What did Jacob promise to give Sulaiman to make up for getting separated?

The etiquette of du'a:

Du'a is a part of worship and like every other kind of worship, the Prophet ﷺ taught us how to perform it with the best of etiquette.

1 – The du'a should be to Allah alone; by obeying Him and not disobeying Him.

2 – When we make du'a we should be sincere in asking Allah, alone.

3 – We should ask of Allah by His most beautiful names.

4 – We should praise Allah as He deserves to be praised before we voice our du'a.

5 – We should send blessings upon the Prophet ﷺ.

6 – We should face towards the qiblah.

7 – Raising our hands together with palms facing upwards in du'a.

8 – We should have certainty that Allah will respond to our du'a.

9 – We should focus on what we are saying and not be distracted when making du'a.

10 – We should ask frequently and not be impatient for Allah to answer.

11 – We should be firm in our du'a. We should not say please grant me if you so wish.

12 – We should call upon Allah in humility, hope and fear.

13 – Ask in du'a three times.

14 – We should make sure our food and clothing are halal and lawful.

15 – It is good to say du'a quietly and not out loud. Allah is All Hearing so we do not need to shout.

Times and places when du'as are answered

There are times when du'as are more likely to be answered. These times include:

1 – Laylat al-Qadar (Month of Ramadan).

2 – Du'a in the last third of the night, before dawn.

3 – Following the prescribed prayers before the salaam.

4 – Between the adhaan and the iqaamah.

5 – When it's raining.

7 – At a certain time on Friday.

9 – When drinking Zamzam water.

10 – When prostrating.

12 – When saying the du'a of Prophet Yunus: ﷺ

"Laa ilaaha illa anta, subhaanaka, inni kuntu min al-zaalimeen ([none has the right to be worshipped but You (O Allah)], Glorified (and Exalted) be You [above all that (evil) they associate with You]! Truly, I have been of the wrongdoers – *surah al-Anbiya'* 21:87)."

13 – If a calamity befalls you and you say, *Inna Lillaahi wa inna ilayhi raaji'oon, Allaahumma ujurni fi museebati w'ukhluf li khayran minha* (Truly, to Allah we belong and truly, to Him we shall return; O Allah, reward me in this calamity and compensate me with something better than it).

14 – The prayer of people after the soul of the deceased has been taken.

15 – Du'a for one who is sick.

16 – The prayer of the one who has been wronged.

17 – The du'a of a father for his child i.e. for their benefit.

18 – The du'a of a fasting person during the day of their fast

19 – The prayer of the traveller.

21 – The du'a of a righteous person for their parents.

22 – Du'a after the sun has passed its zenith and before Dhuhr.

23 – Du'a when getting up from the night (sleep), and saying the du'a that was narrated for that time. *"Laa ilaaha ill-Allah wahdahu la shareeka lah, lahu al-mulku wa lahu al-hamd, wa huwa 'ala kulli shay-in qadeer. Alhamdulillah, wa Subhanallah, wa la ilaha illa Allah wallahu akbar wa laa hawla wa laa quwwata illa Billaah* (There is no god but Allah Alone, He has no partners, His is the Sovereignty, to Him belongs praise and He is over all things Capable. Glory be to Allah, there is no (true) God but Allah, and Allah is Most Great and there is no power and no strength except with Allah), then he says: *Allaahumma ighfir li* (O Allah, forgive me), or he makes du'a, his prayer will be answered, and if he does wudu and prays, his prayer will be accepted."
Narrated by al-Bukhaari, 1154.

Evidence for the story from Hadith

The Prophet ﷺ said, "While three men were walking, it started raining and they took shelter (refuge) in a cave in a mountain. A big rock rolled down from the mountain and closed the mouth of the cave. They said to each other, 'Think of good deeds which you did for Allah's sake only, and invoke Allah by giving reference to those deeds so that He may remove this rock from you.' One of them said, "O Allah! I had old parents and small children and I used to graze the sheep for them. On my return to them in the evening, I used to milk (the sheep) and start providing my parents first of all before my children. One day I was delayed and came late at night and found my parents sleeping. I milked (the sheep) as usual and stood by their heads.

I hated to wake them up and disliked to give milk to my children before them, although my children were weeping (because of hunger) at my feet till the day dawned. O Allah! If I did this for Your sake only, kindly remove the rock so that we could see the sky through it." So, Allah removed the rock a little and they saw the sky. The second man said, 'O Allah! I was in love with a cousin of mine like the deepest love a man may have for a woman.' [He was tested by haram but in the end stayed away from it.] 'O Allah! If I did it for Your sake only, please remove the rock.' The rock shifted a little more. The third man said, 'O Allah! I employed a labourer for a *Faraq* of rice and when he finished his job and demanded his right, I presented it to him, but he refused to take it. So, I sowed the rice many times till I gathered cows and their shepherd (from the yield). (Then after some time) He came and said to me, "Fear Allah (and give me my right)." I said, 'Go and take those cows and the shepherd.' He said, "Be afraid of Allah! Don't mock at me." I said, 'I am not mocking at you. Take (all that).' So, he took all that. O Allah! If I did that for Your sake only, please remove the rest of the rock.' So, Allah removed the rock."

Narrated by Sahih al-Bukhari 2333.

"And if Allah touches you with harm, none can remove it but He, and if He touches you with good, then He is able to do all things."
Surah al-An'am 6:17